TRANSFORMERS
DARK OF THE MOON

VOLUME 2

STORY BY JOHN BARBER
ART BY JORGE JIMENEZ MORENO

COLORS BY ROMULO FAJARDO AND ZAC ATKINSON
LETTERS BY CHRIS MOWRY AND SHAWN LEE
SERIES ASSISTANT EDITOR CARLOS GUZMAN
SERIES EDITOR ANDY SCHMIDT
ADAPTED FROM THE SCREENPLAY BY EHREN KRUGER
COLLECTION EDITOR JUSTIN EISINGER
COLLECTION DESIGNER SHAWN LEE

Licensed By:
GM Hasbro Paramount IDW Spotlight

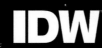

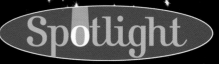

visit us at www.abdopublishing.com

Reinforced library bound edition published in 2012 by Spotlight,
a division of the ABDO Group, PO Box 398166, Minneapolis, MN 55439.
Spotlight produces high-quality reinforced library bound editions for schools and libraries. Published by agreement with IDW Publishing. www.idwpublishing.com

Printed in the United States of America, North Mankato, Minnesota.
102011
012012
This book contains at least 10% recycled materials.

Cataloging-in-Publication Data

Barber, John, 1976-
Transformers: Dark of the moon / story by John Barber ; art by Jorge Jimenez Moreno
p. cm. -- (Transformers, dark of the moon movie adaptation)
ISBN 978-1-59961-966-8 (volume 1) -- ISBN 978-1-59961-967-5 (volume 2) -- ISBN 978-1-59961-968-2 (volume 3) -- ISBN 978-1-59961-969-9 (volume 4)
1. Graphic novels. II. Moreno, Jorge Jimenez, III. Transformers, dark of the moon (Motion picture) IV. Title.
PZ7.7.B35Tr 2012
741.5'973--dc23

Spotlight

All Spotlight books are reinforced library binding and manufactured in the United States of America.

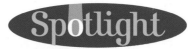

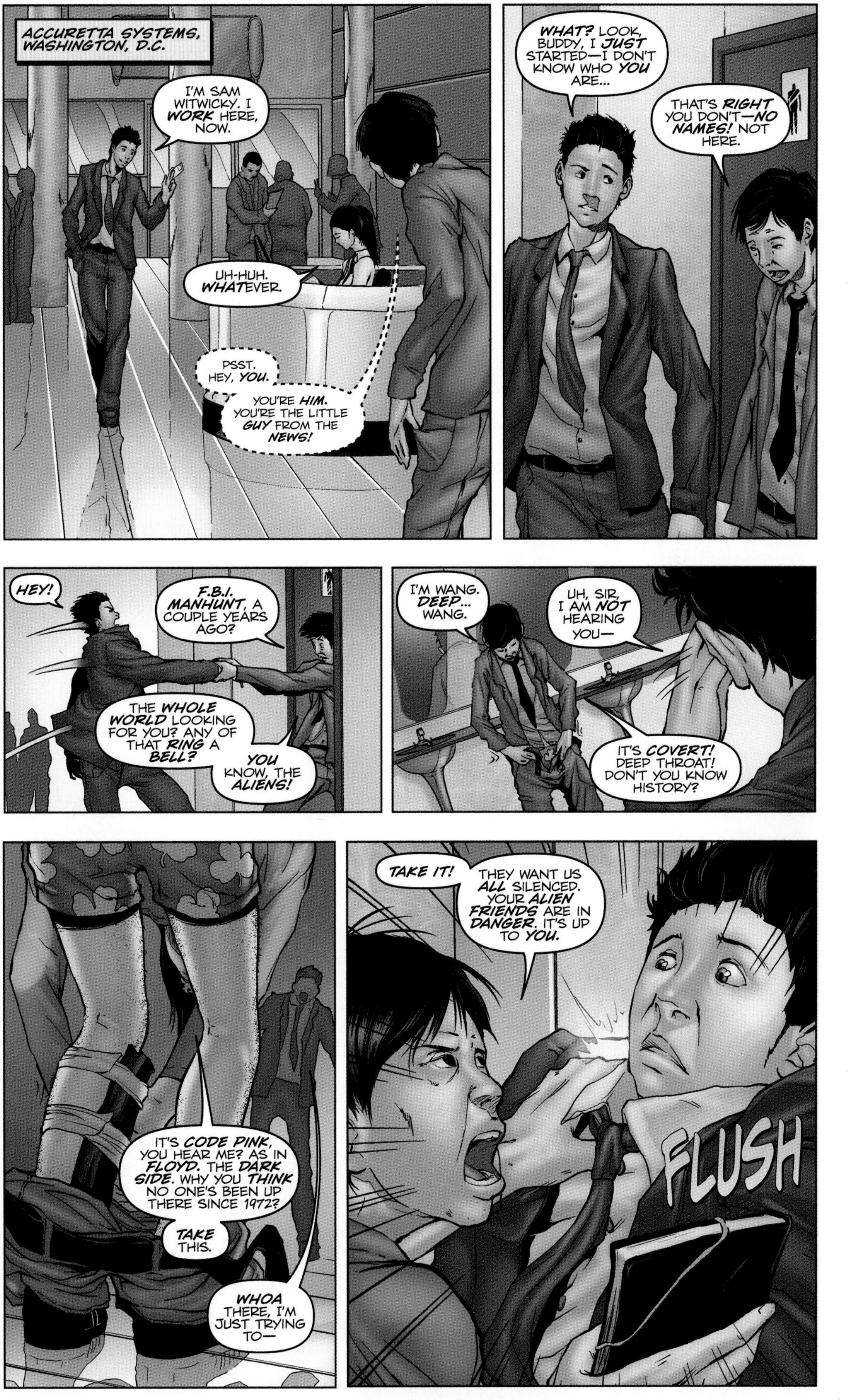
ACCURETTA SYSTEMS, WASHINGTON, D.C.
I'M SAM WITWICKY. I WORK HERE, NOW.
UH-HUH. WHATEVER.
PSST. HEY, YOU.
YOU'RE HIM. YOU'RE THE LITTLE GUY FROM THE NEWS!
WHAT? LOOK, BUDDY, I JUST STARTED—I DON'T KNOW WHO YOU ARE...
THAT'S RIGHT YOU DON'T—NO NAMES! NOT HERE.
HEY!
F.B.I. MANHUNT, A COUPLE YEARS AGO?
THE WHOLE WORLD LOOKING FOR YOU? ANY OF THAT RING A BELL?
YOU KNOW, THE ALIENS!
I'M WANG. DEEP... WANG.
UH, SIR, I AM NOT HEARING YOU—
IT'S COVERT! DEEP THROAT! DON'T YOU KNOW HISTORY?
IT'S CODE PINK, YOU HEAR ME? AS IN FLOYD. THE DARK SIDE. WHY YOU THINK NO ONE'S BEEN UP THERE SINCE 1972?
TAKE THIS.
WHOA THERE, I'M JUST TRYING TO—
TAKE IT!
THEY WANT US ALL SILENCED. YOUR ALIEN FRIENDS ARE IN DANGER. IT'S UP TO YOU.
FLUSH

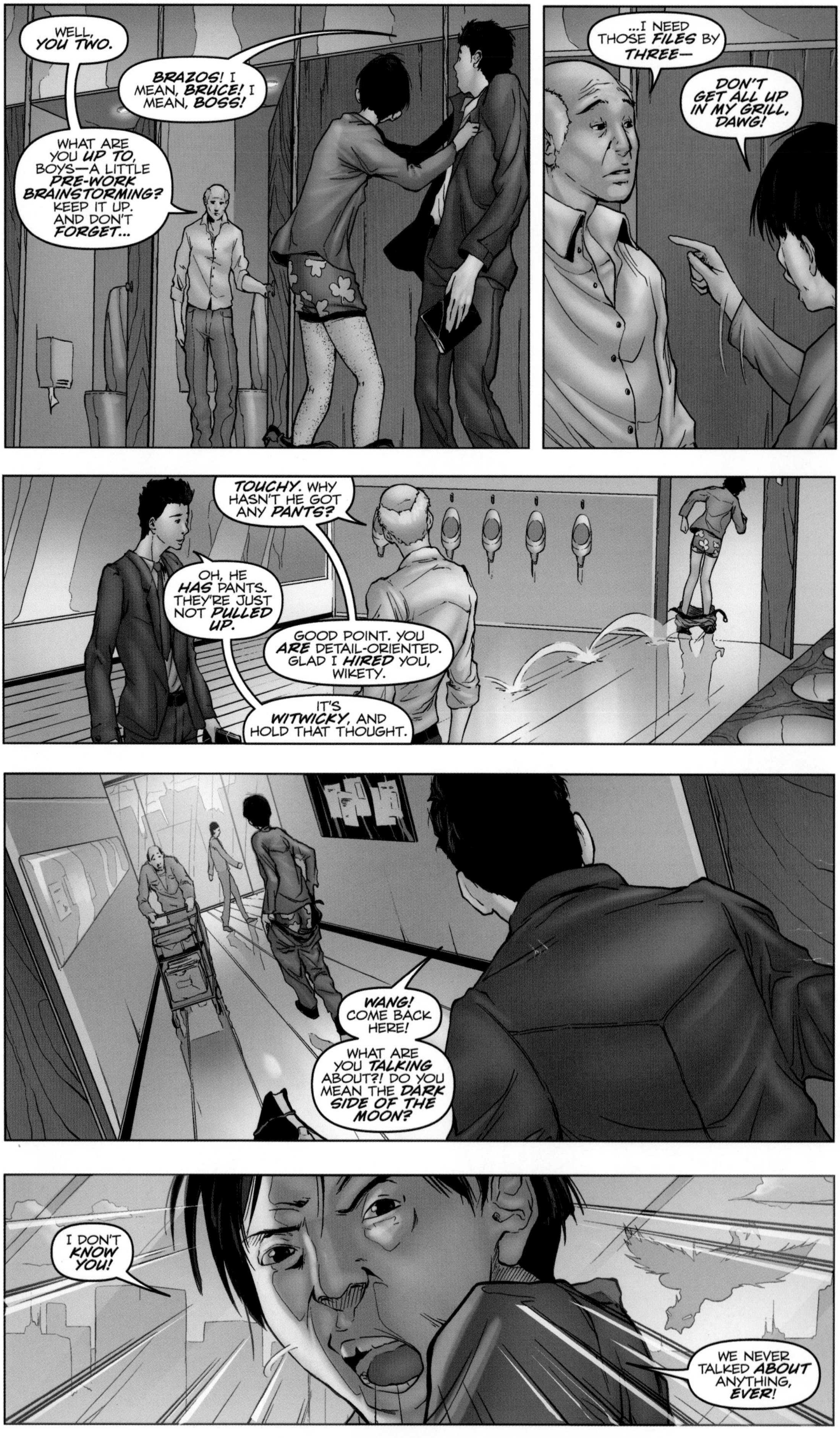
WELL, YOU TWO.
BRAZOS! I MEAN, BRUCE! I MEAN, BOSS!
WHAT ARE YOU UP TO, BOYS—A LITTLE PRE-WORK BRAINSTORMING? KEEP IT UP. AND DON'T FORGET...
...I NEED THOSE FILES BY THREE—
DON'T GET ALL UP IN MY GRILL, DAWG!
TOUCHY. WHY HASN'T HE GOT ANY PANTS?
OH, HE HAS PANTS. THEY'RE JUST NOT PULLED UP.
GOOD POINT. YOU ARE DETAIL-ORIENTED. GLAD I HIRED YOU, WIKETY.
IT'S WITWICKY, AND HOLD THAT THOUGHT.
WANG! COME BACK HERE!
WHAT ARE YOU TALKING ABOUT?! DO YOU MEAN THE DARK SIDE OF THE MOON?
I DON'T KNOW YOU!
WE NEVER TALKED ABOUT ANYTHING, EVER!

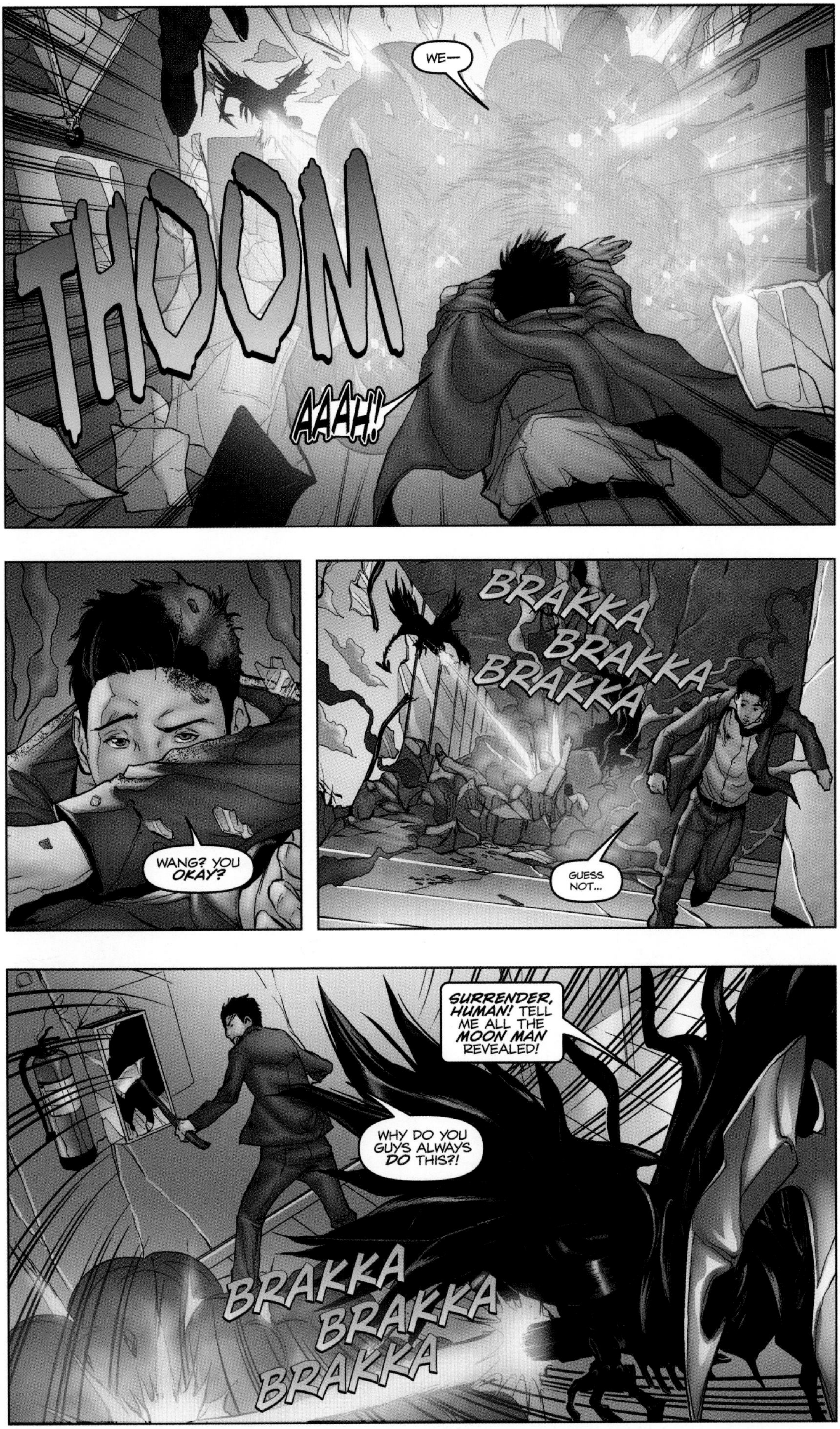
WE—
THOOM
AAAH!
WANG? YOU OKAY?
BRAKKA BRAKKA BRAKKA
GUESS NOT...
SURRENDER, HUMAN! TELL ME ALL THE MOON MAN REVEALED!
WHY DO YOU GUYS ALWAYS DO THIS?!
BRAKKA BRAKKA BRAKKA

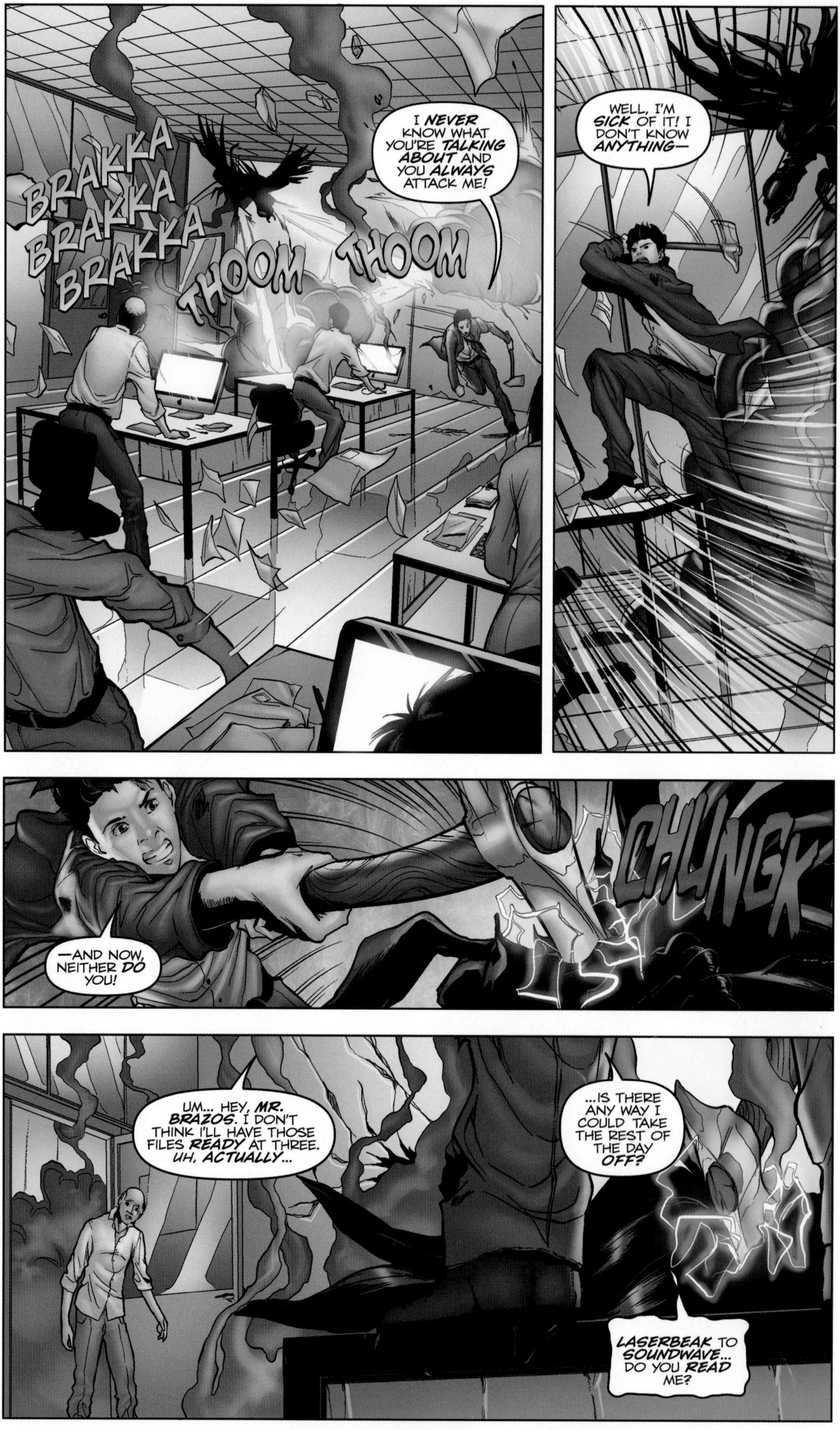
I NEVER KNOW WHAT YOU'RE TALKING ABOUT AND YOU ALWAYS ATTACK ME!
BRAKKA BRAKKA BRAKKA
THOOM THOOM
WELL, I'M SICK OF IT! I DON'T KNOW ANYTHING—
CHUNGK
—AND NOW, NEITHER DO YOU!
UM... HEY, MR. BRAZOS. I DON'T THINK I'LL HAVE THOSE FILES READY AT THREE. UH, ACTUALLY...
...IS THERE ANY WAY I COULD TAKE THE REST OF THE DAY OFF?
LASERBEAK TO SOUNDWAVE... DO YOU READ ME?

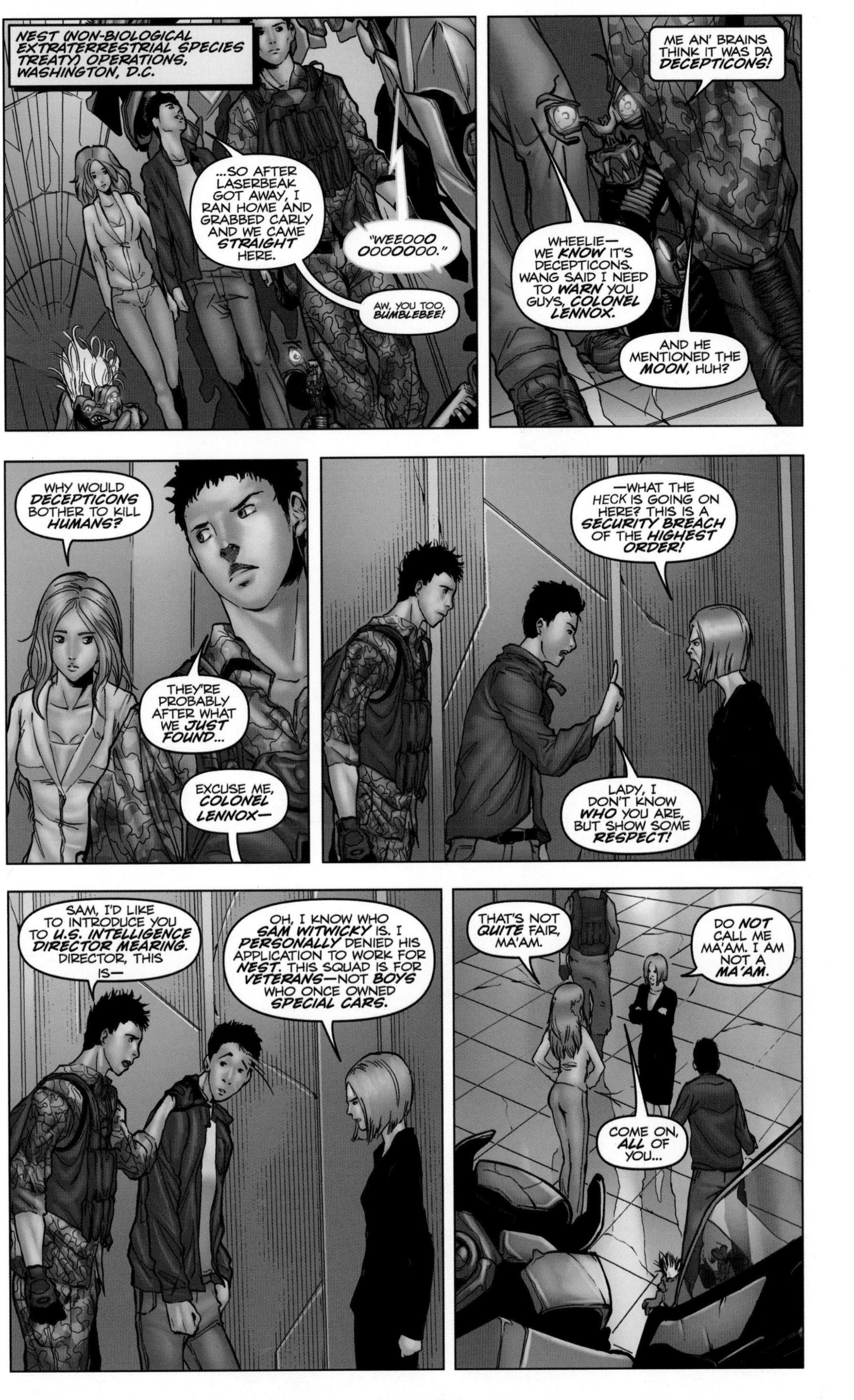
NEST (NON-BIOLOGICAL EXTRATERRESTRIAL SPECIES TREATY) OPERATIONS, WASHINGTON, D.C.
...SO AFTER LASERBEAK GOT AWAY, I RAN HOME AND GRABBED CARLY AND WE CAME STRAIGHT HERE.
"WEEOOO OOOOOOO."
AW, YOU TOO, BUMBLEBEE!
ME AN' BRAINS THINK IT WAS DA DECEPTICONS!
WHEELIE— WE KNOW IT'S DECEPTICONS. WANG SAID I NEED TO WARN YOU GUYS, COLONEL LENNOX.
AND HE MENTIONED THE MOON, HUH?
WHY WOULD DECEPTICONS BOTHER TO KILL HUMANS?
THEY'RE PROBABLY AFTER WHAT WE JUST FOUND...
EXCUSE ME, COLONEL LENNOX—
—WHAT THE HECK IS GOING ON HERE? THIS IS A SECURITY BREACH OF THE HIGHEST ORDER!
LADY, I DON'T KNOW WHO YOU ARE, BUT SHOW SOME RESPECT!
SAM, I'D LIKE TO INTRODUCE YOU TO U.S. INTELLIGENCE DIRECTOR MEARING. DIRECTOR, THIS IS—
OH, I KNOW WHO SAM WITWICKY IS. I PERSONALLY DENIED HIS APPLICATION TO WORK FOR NEST. THIS SQUAD IS FOR VETERANS—NOT BOYS WHO ONCE OWNED SPECIAL CARS.
THAT'S NOT QUITE FAIR, MA'AM.
DO NOT CALL ME MA'AM. I AM NOT A MA'AM.
COME ON, ALL OF YOU...

...YOU NEED TO SEE THIS.

HELLO, SAMUEL.

IRONHIDE, RATCHET! WHAT'S... OH... WHO...?

I SUPPOSE I COULD BE JEALOUS OF THEM.

AFTER ALL, THE AUTOBOTS HAVE FRIENDS.

THAT'S SENTINEL PRIME.

HE WAS OPTIMUS' MENTOR, AND... HE ONCE WAS OUR LEADER.

THE MATRIX OF LEADERSHIP—THE ONLY THING IN THE UNIVERSE THAT COULD POSSIBLY RE-POWER AN AUTOBOT THAT'S BEEN STUCK ON THE MOON FOR SO LONG.

THE MOON, COLONEL LENNOX?

SHH, SAM. THIS IS A SOLEMN MOMENT.

I TAKE SOLACE THAT ONLY FRIENDS...

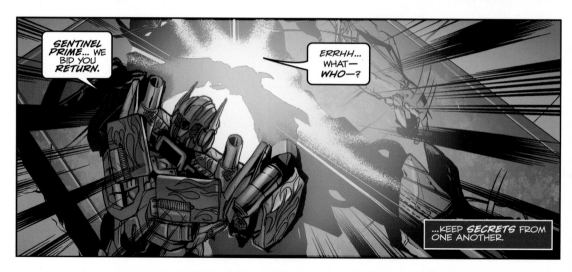

SENTINEL PRIME... WE BID YOU RETURN.

ERRHH... WHAT— WHO—?

...KEEP SECRETS FROM ONE ANOTHER.

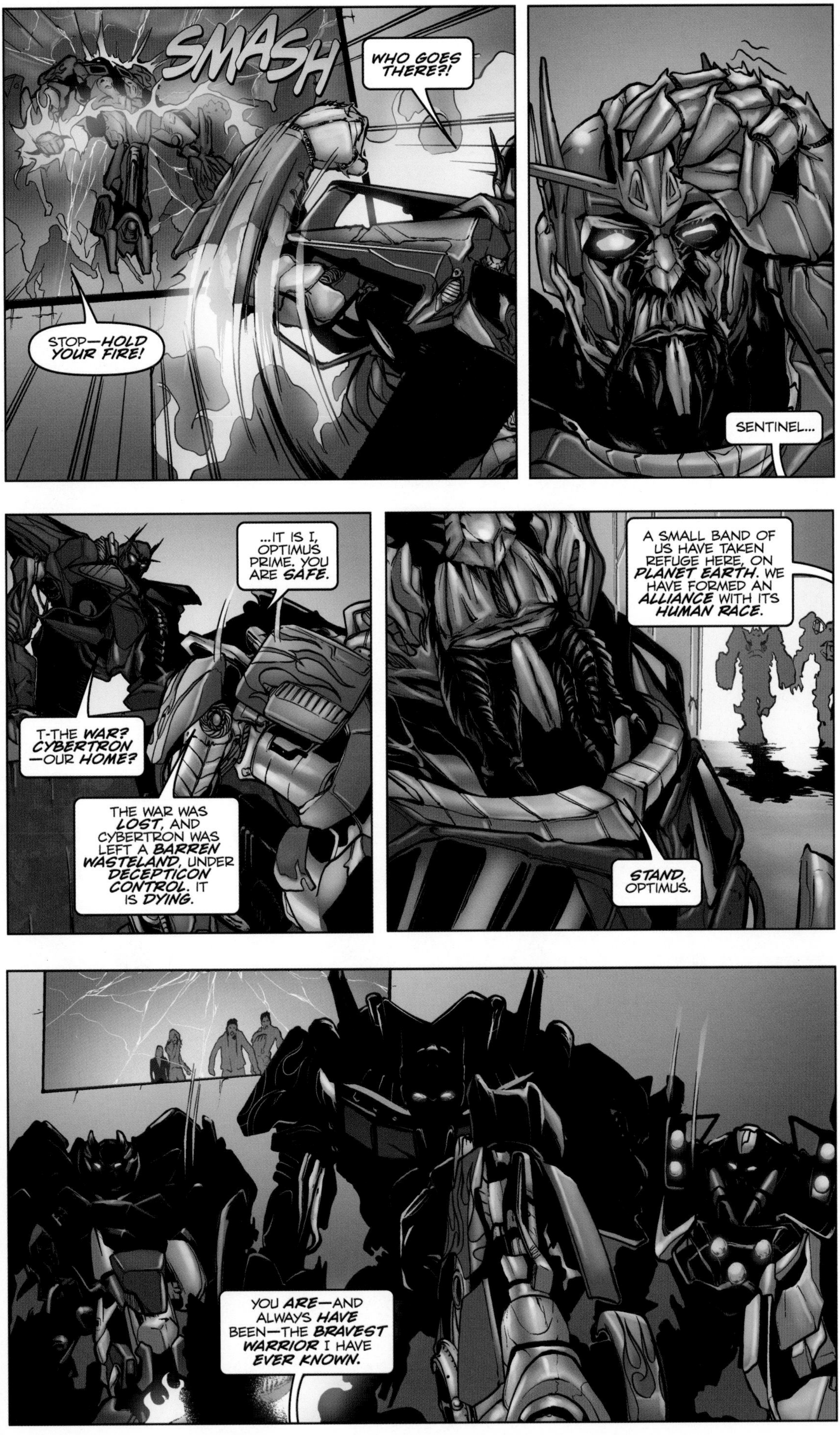
SMASH
WHO GOES THERE?!
STOP—HOLD YOUR FIRE!
SENTINEL...
...IT IS I, OPTIMUS PRIME. YOU ARE SAFE.
T-THE WAR? CYBERTRON —OUR HOME?
THE WAR WAS LOST, AND CYBERTRON WAS LEFT A BARREN WASTELAND, UNDER DECEPTICON CONTROL. IT IS DYING.
A SMALL BAND OF US HAVE TAKEN REFUGE HERE, ON PLANET EARTH. WE HAVE FORMED AN ALLIANCE WITH ITS HUMAN RACE.
STAND, OPTIMUS.
YOU ARE—AND ALWAYS HAVE BEEN—THE BRAVEST WARRIOR I HAVE EVER KNOWN.

ON CYBERTRON, I MOVED TO *END* THE *WAR*... MY SHIP WAS *DAMAGED*...

WE THOUGHT YOU WERE *DESTROYED*— BUT YOU SAVED FIVE *PILLARS*, SENTINEL.

ONLY *FIVE*... ONCE WE HAD *HUNDREDS*...

AUTOBOTS. WHAT IS THIS *TECHNOLOGY* YOU'RE TALKING ABOUT?

SHE IS ONE OF OUR *ALLIES.* WE CAN TRUST *HER.*

TOGETHER, THE *PILLARS* FORM A *SPACE BRIDGE.*

I *DESIGNED* IT, AND I *ALONE* CAN CONTROL IT. IT DEFIES THE LAWS OF *PHYSICS* TO *TRANSPORT MATTER* THROUGH *TIME* AND *SPACE.* IT WAS TO BE OUR KEY TO *WINNING THE WAR*...

YOU'RE TALKING ABOUT *TELEPORTATION.*

FOR *RESOURCES.* REFUGEES.

OR *SOLDIERS.* WEAPONS, BOMBS—IT'S A MEANS OF *INSTANT STRIKE.*

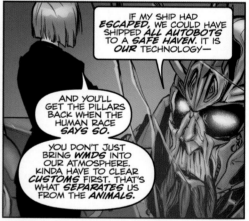

IF MY SHIP HAD *ESCAPED,* WE COULD HAVE SHIPPED *ALL AUTOBOTS* TO A *SAFE HAVEN.* IT IS *OUR* TECHNOLOGY—

AND YOU'LL GET THE PILLARS BACK WHEN THE HUMAN RACE *SAYS SO.*

YOU DON'T JUST BRING *WMDS* INTO OUR ATMOSPHERE. KINDA HAVE TO CLEAR *CUSTOMS* FIRST. THAT'S WHAT *SEPARATES* US FROM THE *ANIMALS.*

I AM *GRATEFUL* FOR YOUR ALLIANCE. BUT *HEAR ME* AND *MARK MY WORDS*—THE *DECEPTICONS* MUST *NEVER KNOW* THE SPACE BRIDGE IS *HERE.* FOR IN *THEIR* HANDS...

...IT WOULD MEAN THE *END* OF YOUR WORLD.

SECRETS.

SECRETS AND *FRIENDS*. EVENTS ARE IN MOTION, AND NOT EVEN I CAN STOP THEM NOW.

NAMIBIA, AFRICA.

RARF! MASTER!

SILENCE, IGOR. I HAVE *BUSINESS.*

LORD MEGATRON.

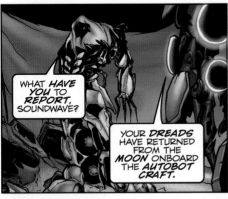

WHAT *HAVE YOU* TO *REPORT,* SOUNDWAVE?

YOUR *DREADS* HAVE RETURNED FROM THE *MOON* ONBOARD THE *AUTOBOT CRAFT.*

WHAT YOU *BELIEVED* WOULD HAPPEN...

HAS HAPPENED. SEND THE DREADS TO THE *SECONDARY OBJECTIVE* AND GATHER MY *TROOPS,* SOUNDWAVE.

I RULE THE *DECEPTICON EMPIRE.*

I SHALL *CARVE* THE NAME *"MEGATRON"* INTO THE VERY *FABRIC* OF THE *UNIVERSE,* SO *NONE* SHALL EVER *FORGET ME.*

WHAT USE WOULD ONE SUCH AS *I* HAVE...

...FOR *FRIENDS?*

SEVEN HUNDRED *THIRTEEN,* SEVEN HUNDRED *FOURTEEN...*

YOU *COUNTED* THAT STAR ALREADY!

DID *NOT!* THAT'S SEVEN HUNDRED AN'... AW, HECK, I LOST *TRACK...*

I CAN'T *BELIEVE* THEY SIDELINED ME *AGAIN...*

SAM WITWICKY'S APARTMENT, WASHINGTON, D.C.

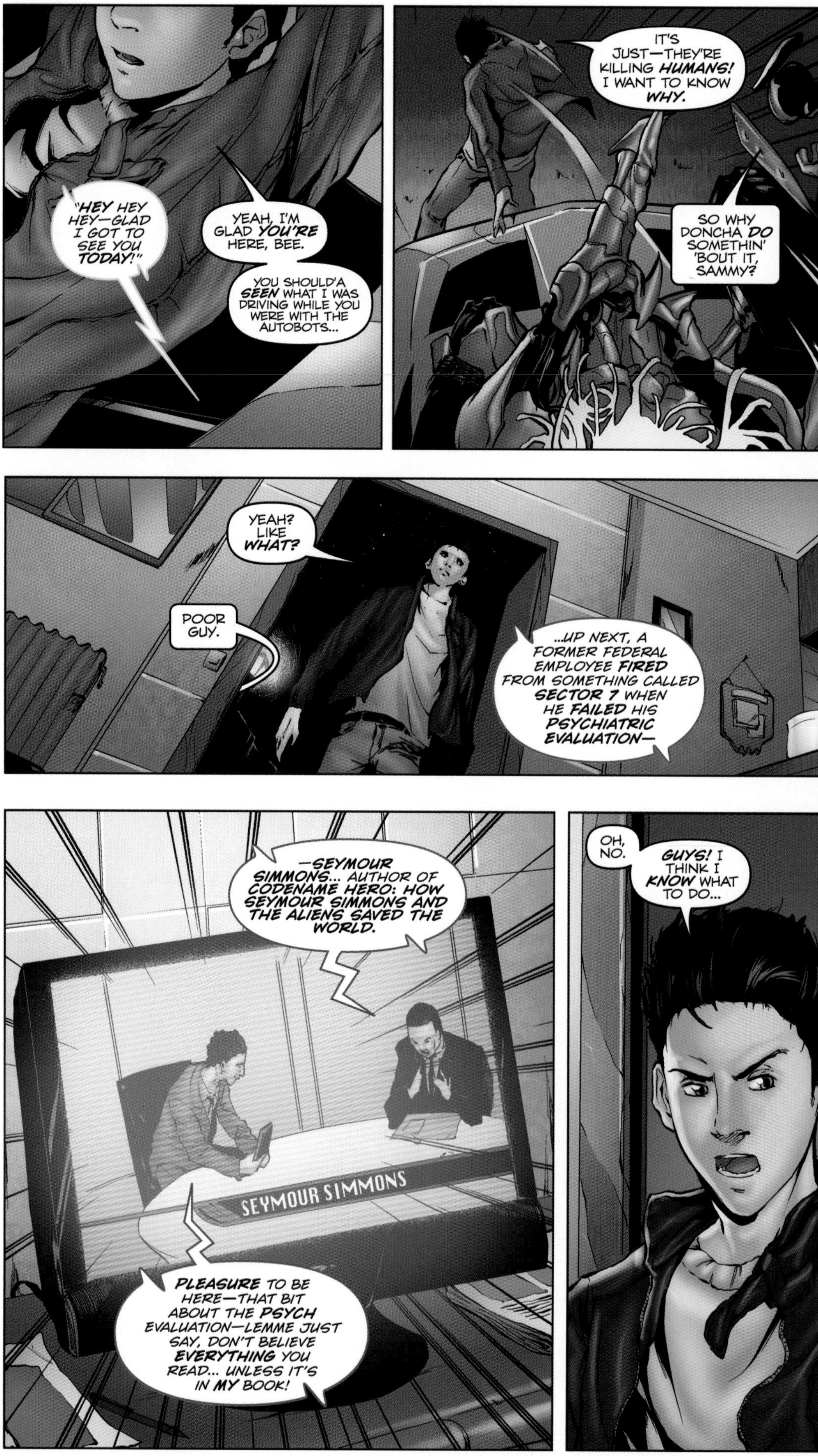

"HEY HEY HEY—GLAD I GOT TO SEE YOU TODAY!"
YEAH, I'M GLAD YOU'RE HERE, BEE.
YOU SHOULD'A SEEN WHAT I WAS DRIVING WHILE YOU WERE WITH THE AUTOBOTS...
IT'S JUST—THEY'RE KILLING HUMANS! I WANT TO KNOW WHY.
SO WHY DONCHA DO SOMETHIN' 'BOUT IT, SAMMY?
YEAH? LIKE WHAT?
POOR GUY.
...UP NEXT, A FORMER FEDERAL EMPLOYEE FIRED FROM SOMETHING CALLED SECTOR 7 WHEN HE FAILED HIS PSYCHIATRIC EVALUATION—
—SEYMOUR SIMMONS... AUTHOR OF CODENAME HERO: HOW SEYMOUR SIMMONS AND THE ALIENS SAVED THE WORLD.
SEYMOUR SIMMONS
PLEASURE TO BE HERE—THAT BIT ABOUT THE PSYCH EVALUATION—LEMME JUST SAY, DON'T BELIEVE EVERYTHING YOU READ... UNLESS IT'S IN MY BOOK!
OH, NO.
GUYS! I THINK I KNOW WHAT TO DO...

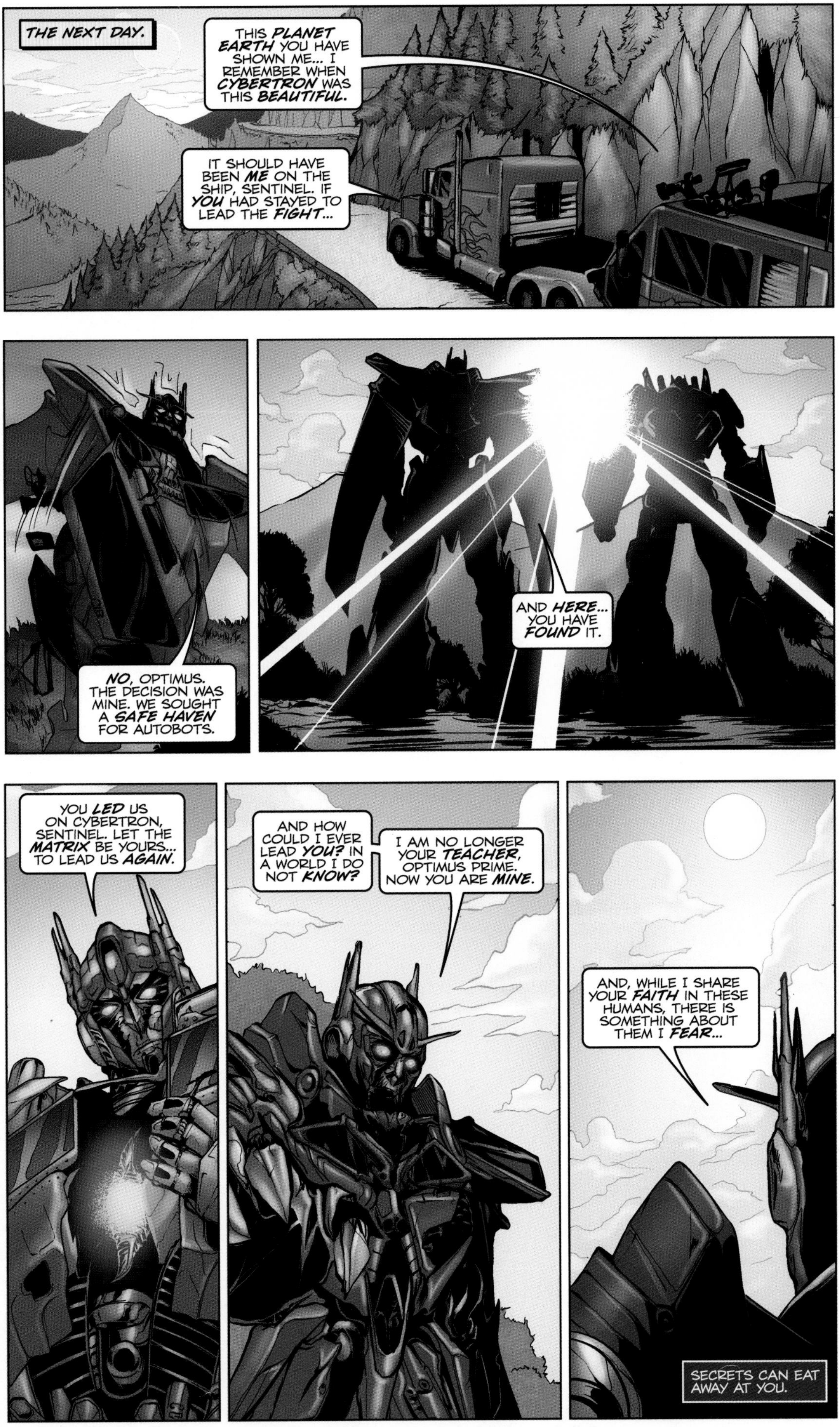
THE NEXT DAY.
THIS PLANET EARTH YOU HAVE SHOWN ME... I REMEMBER WHEN CYBERTRON WAS THIS BEAUTIFUL.
IT SHOULD HAVE BEEN ME ON THE SHIP, SENTINEL. IF YOU HAD STAYED TO LEAD THE FIGHT...
NO, OPTIMUS. THE DECISION WAS MINE. WE SOUGHT A SAFE HAVEN FOR AUTOBOTS.
AND HERE... YOU HAVE FOUND IT.
YOU LED US ON CYBERTRON, SENTINEL. LET THE MATRIX BE YOURS... TO LEAD US AGAIN.
AND HOW COULD I EVER LEAD YOU? IN A WORLD I DO NOT KNOW?
I AM NO LONGER YOUR TEACHER, OPTIMUS PRIME. NOW YOU ARE MINE.
AND, WHILE I SHARE YOUR FAITH IN THESE HUMANS, THERE IS SOMETHING ABOUT THEM I FEAR...
SECRETS CAN EAT AWAY AT YOU.

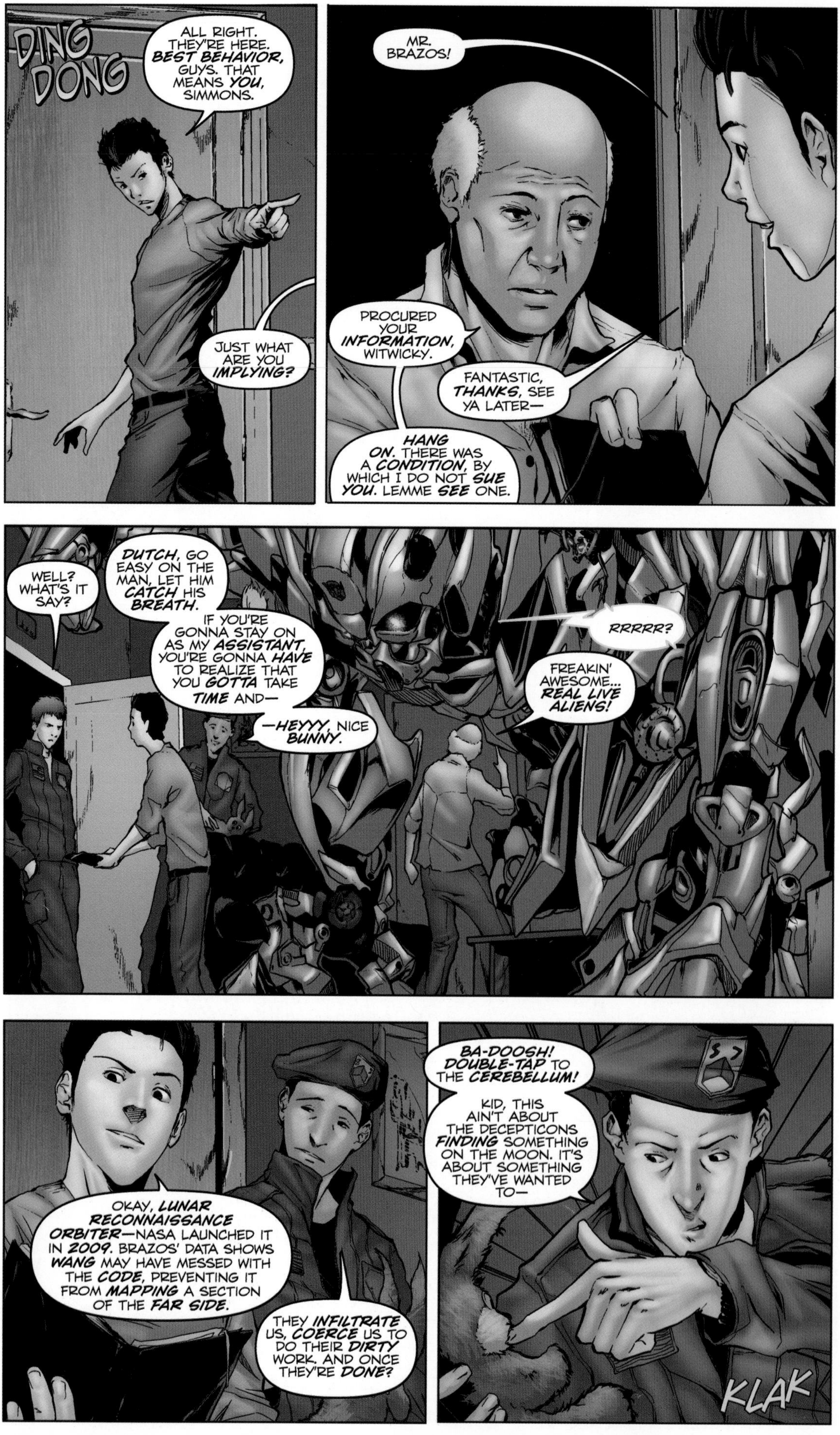
DING DONG
ALL RIGHT. THEY'RE HERE. BEST BEHAVIOR, GUYS. THAT MEANS YOU, SIMMONS.
JUST WHAT ARE YOU IMPLYING?
MR. BRAZOS!
PROCURED YOUR INFORMATION, WITWICKY.
FANTASTIC, THANKS, SEE YA LATER—
HANG ON. THERE WAS A CONDITION, BY WHICH I DO NOT SUE YOU. LEMME SEE ONE.
WELL? WHAT'S IT SAY?
DUTCH, GO EASY ON THE MAN, LET HIM CATCH HIS BREATH.
IF YOU'RE GONNA STAY ON AS MY ASSISTANT, YOU'RE GONNA HAVE TO REALIZE THAT YOU GOTTA TAKE TIME AND—
—HEYYY, NICE BUNNY.
RRRRR?
FREAKIN' AWESOME... REAL LIVE ALIENS!
OKAY, LUNAR RECONNAISSANCE ORBITER—NASA LAUNCHED IT IN 2009. BRAZOS' DATA SHOWS WANG MAY HAVE MESSED WITH THE CODE, PREVENTING IT FROM MAPPING A SECTION OF THE FAR SIDE.
THEY INFILTRATE US, COERCE US TO DO THEIR DIRTY WORK. AND ONCE THEY'RE DONE?
BA-DOOSH! DOUBLE-TAP TO THE CEREBELLUM!
KID, THIS AIN'T ABOUT THE DECEPTICONS FINDING SOMETHING ON THE MOON. IT'S ABOUT SOMETHING THEY'VE WANTED TO—
KLAK

—HIDE. WHO ARE *YOU*? WHO *IS* THAT? GET HER *OUT OF HERE*!

CARLY! ER—I DIDN'T HEAR YOU!

I CAME IN THROUGH THE *KITCHEN*, SAM! WHAT'S GOING ON—DID YOU *FORGET*?

IT'S *SATURDAY*. WE'RE SUPPOSED TO BE AT *DYLAN'S PARTY*. I *TOLD* YOU ABOUT IT—IT'S FOR *MY JOB*. THE ONE THAT *PAYS* THE BILLS.

YOU TOLD ME WE WERE *DONE* WITH THIS, AFTER WHAT HAPPENED, BACK AT YOUR *SCHOOL*. YOU SAID ALL YOUR *LIFE-AND-DEATH* STUFF WAS *OVER*.

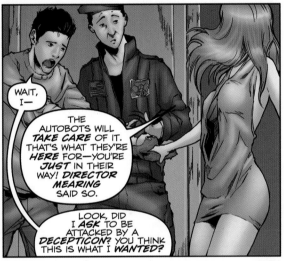

WAIT, I—

THE AUTOBOTS WILL *TAKE CARE* OF IT. THAT'S WHAT THEY'RE *HERE* FOR—YOU'RE *JUST* IN THEIR WAY! *DIRECTOR MEARING* SAID SO.

LOOK, DID I *ASK* TO BE ATTACKED BY A *DECEPTICON*? YOU THINK THIS IS WHAT I *WANTED*?

YES. YES, I *DO*.

RRIP

SO *GOOD LUCK*. I GOTTA *GO*.

SLAM *CARLY!*

YOU'RE *BETTER OFF* THIS WAY, KID. THE *WARRIOR'S PATH* IS A *SOLITARY* ONE—TAKE IT FROM *ME*.

I STILL DON'T *GET* THE THING WITH THE *STUFFED BUNNY*.

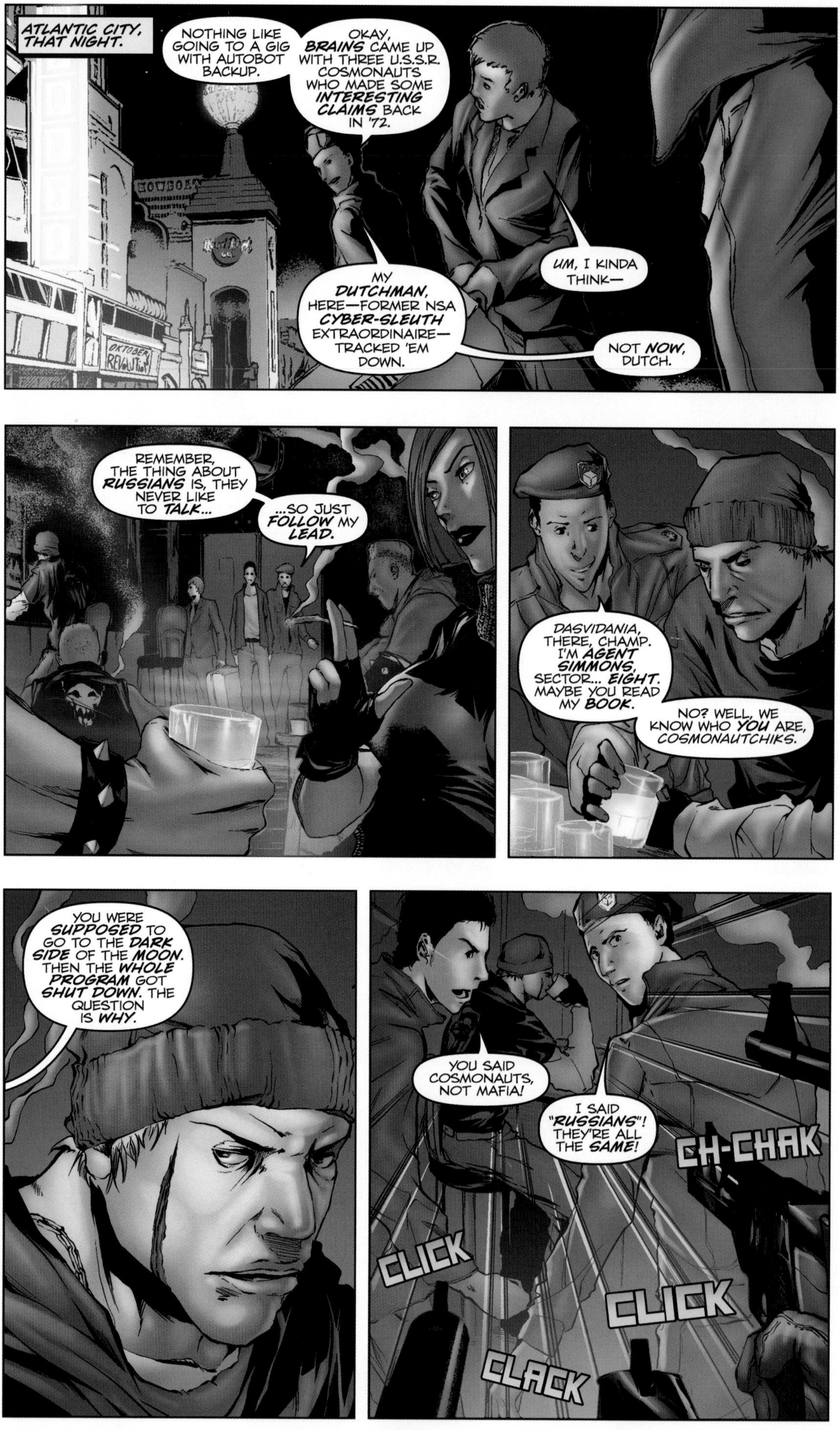
ATLANTIC CITY, THAT NIGHT.
NOTHING LIKE GOING TO A GIG WITH AUTOBOT BACKUP.
OKAY, BRAINS CAME UP WITH THREE U.S.S.R. COSMONAUTS WHO MADE SOME INTERESTING CLAIMS BACK IN '72.
MY DUTCHMAN, HERE—FORMER NSA CYBER-SLEUTH EXTRAORDINAIRE—TRACKED 'EM DOWN.
UM, I KINDA THINK—
NOT NOW, DUTCH.
REMEMBER, THE THING ABOUT RUSSIANS IS, THEY NEVER LIKE TO TALK...
...SO JUST FOLLOW MY LEAD.
DASVIDANIA, THERE, CHAMP. I'M AGENT SIMMONS, SECTOR... EIGHT. MAYBE YOU READ MY BOOK.
NO? WELL, WE KNOW WHO YOU ARE, COSMONAUTCHIKS.
YOU WERE SUPPOSED TO GO TO THE DARK SIDE OF THE MOON. THEN THE WHOLE PROGRAM GOT SHUT DOWN. THE QUESTION IS WHY.
YOU SAID COSMONAUTS, NOT MAFIA!
I SAID "RUSSIANS"! THEY'RE ALL THE SAME!
CH-CHAK
CLICK
CLICK
CLACK

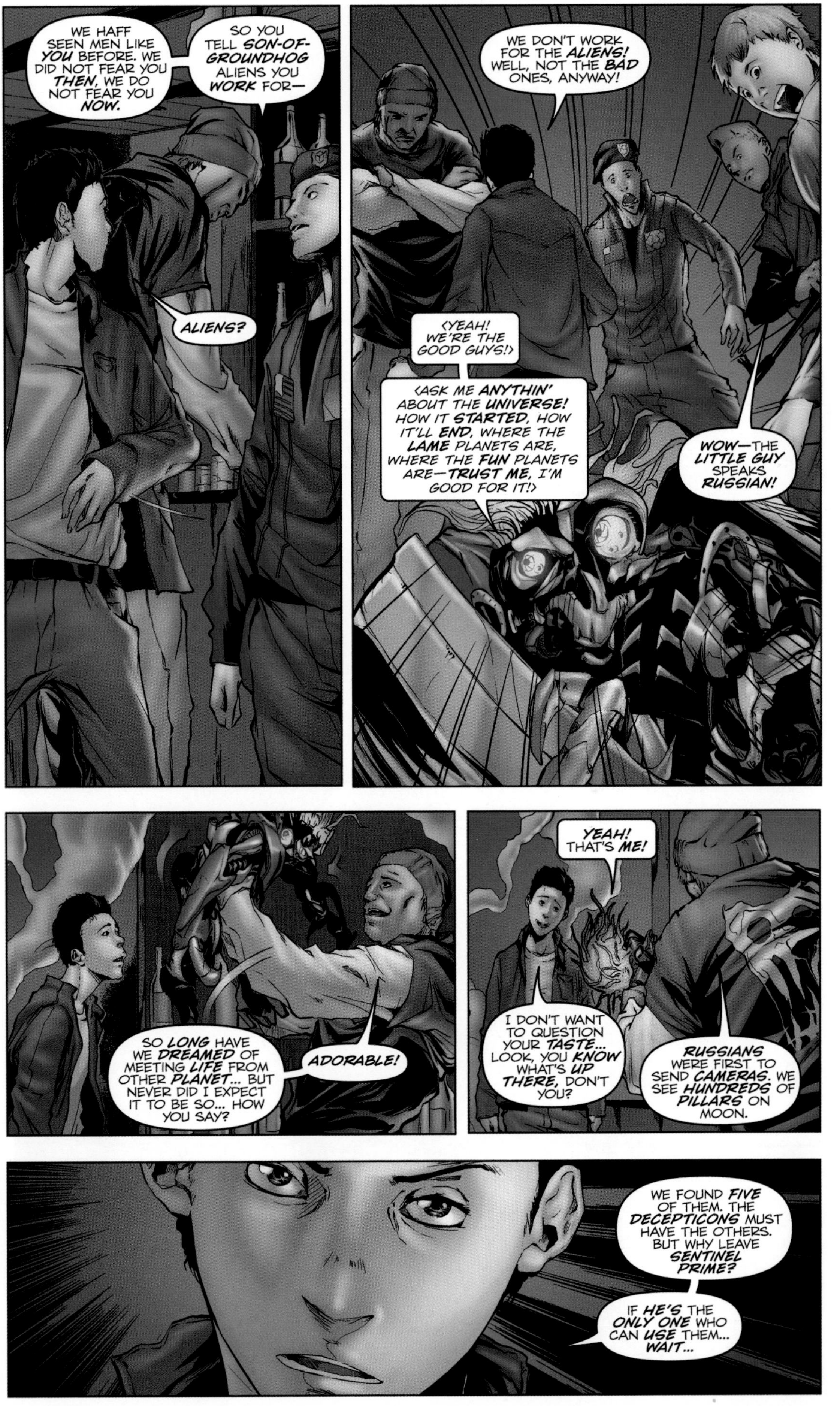
WE HAFF SEEN MEN LIKE YOU BEFORE. WE DID NOT FEAR YOU THEN, WE DO NOT FEAR YOU NOW.
SO YOU TELL SON-OF-GROUNDHOG ALIENS YOU WORK FOR—
ALIENS?
WE DON'T WORK FOR THE ALIENS! WELL, NOT THE BAD ONES, ANYWAY!
<YEAH! WE'RE THE GOOD GUYS!>
<ASK ME ANYTHIN' ABOUT THE UNIVERSE! HOW IT STARTED, HOW IT'LL END, WHERE THE LAME PLANETS ARE, WHERE THE FUN PLANETS ARE—TRUST ME, I'M GOOD FOR IT!>
WOW—THE LITTLE GUY SPEAKS RUSSIAN!
SO LONG HAVE WE DREAMED OF MEETING LIFE FROM OTHER PLANET... BUT NEVER DID I EXPECT IT TO BE SO... HOW YOU SAY?
ADORABLE!
YEAH! THAT'S ME!
I DON'T WANT TO QUESTION YOUR TASTE... LOOK, YOU KNOW WHAT'S UP THERE, DON'T YOU?
RUSSIANS WERE FIRST TO SEND CAMERAS. WE SEE HUNDREDS OF PILLARS ON MOON.
WE FOUND FIVE OF THEM. THE DECEPTICONS MUST HAVE THE OTHERS. BUT WHY LEAVE SENTINEL PRIME?
IF HE'S THE ONLY ONE WHO CAN USE THEM... WAIT...

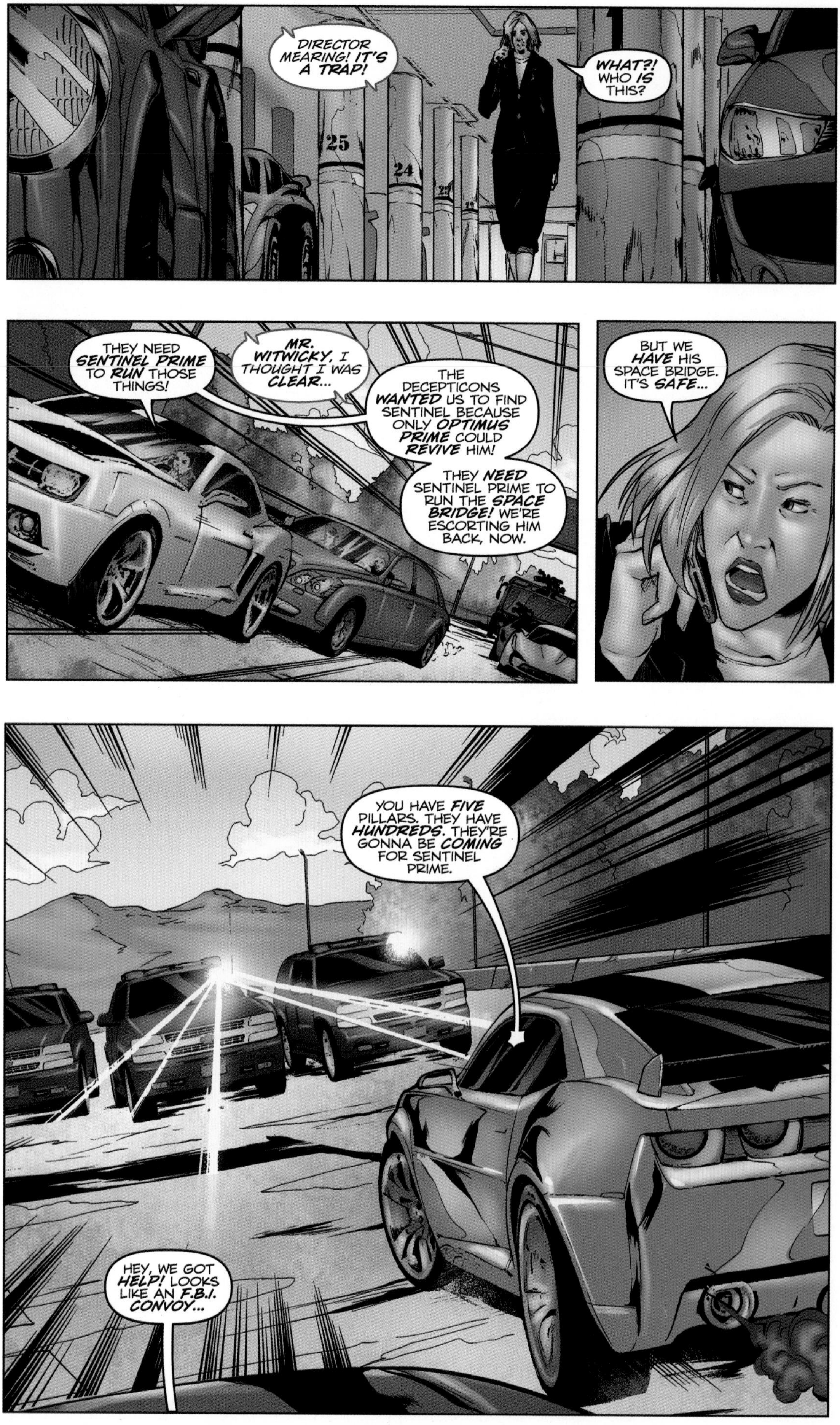

DIRECTOR MEARING! IT'S A TRAP!
WHAT?! WHO IS THIS?
THEY NEED SENTINEL PRIME TO RUN THOSE THINGS!
MR. WITWICKY, I THOUGHT I WAS CLEAR...
THE DECEPTICONS WANTED US TO FIND SENTINEL BECAUSE ONLY OPTIMUS PRIME COULD REVIVE HIM!
THEY NEED SENTINEL PRIME TO RUN THE SPACE BRIDGE! WE'RE ESCORTING HIM BACK, NOW.
BUT WE HAVE HIS SPACE BRIDGE. IT'S SAFE...
YOU HAVE FIVE PILLARS. THEY HAVE HUNDREDS. THEY'RE GONNA BE COMING FOR SENTINEL PRIME.
HEY, WE GOT HELP! LOOKS LIKE AN F.B.I. CONVOY...

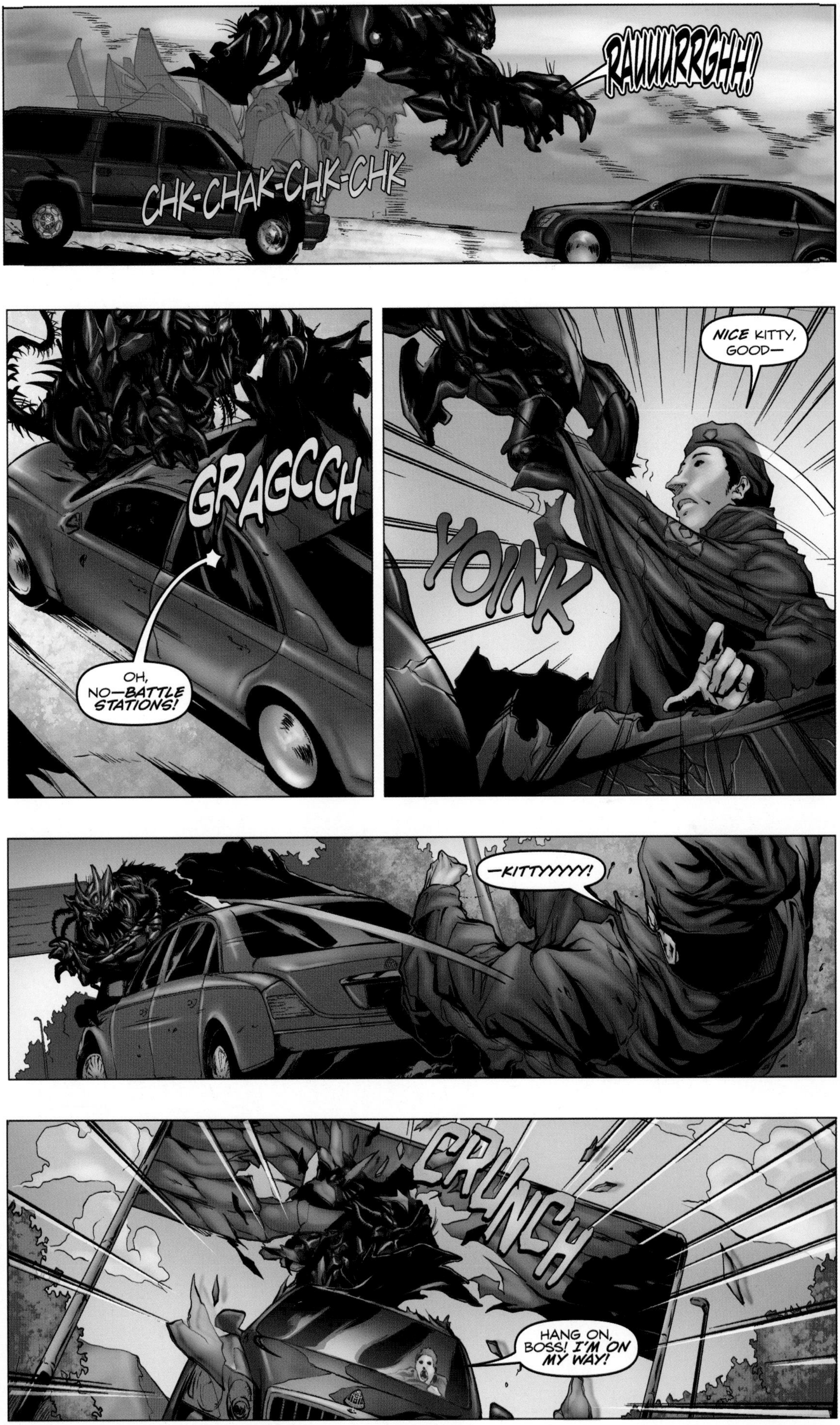
RAUUURRGHH!
CHK-CHAK-CHK-CHK
GRAGCCH
OH, NO—BATTLE STATIONS!
NICE KITTY, GOOD—
YOINK
—KITTYYYYY!
CRUNCH
HANG ON, BOSS! I'M ON MY WAY!

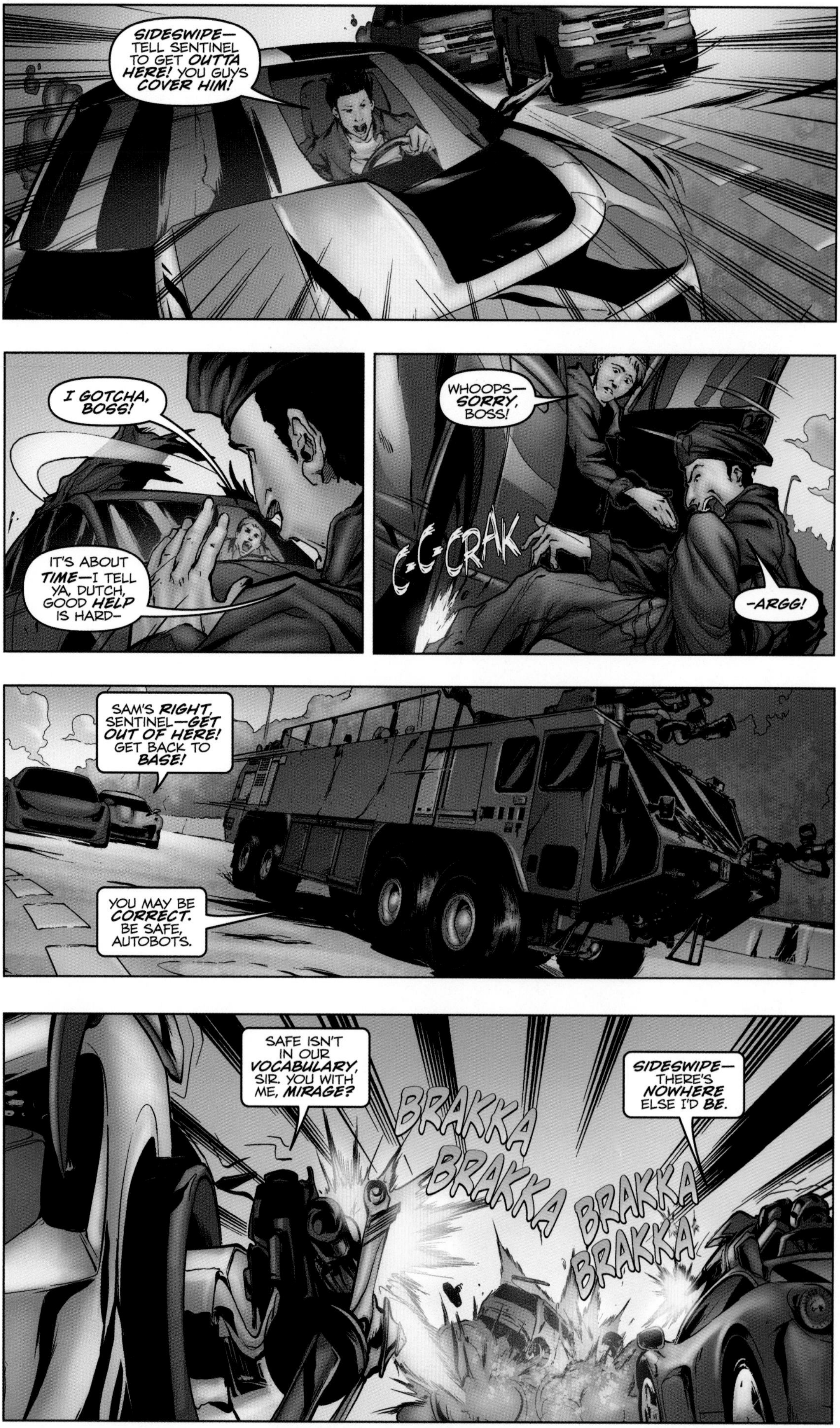

SIDESWIPE—TELL SENTINEL TO GET OUTTA HERE! YOU GUYS COVER HIM!
I GOTCHA, BOSS!
IT'S ABOUT TIME—I TELL YA, DUTCH, GOOD HELP IS HARD-
WHOOPS—SORRY, BOSS!
C-C-CRAK
-ARGG!
SAM'S RIGHT, SENTINEL—GET OUT OF HERE! GET BACK TO BASE!
YOU MAY BE CORRECT. BE SAFE, AUTOBOTS.
SAFE ISN'T IN OUR VOCABULARY, SIR. YOU WITH ME, MIRAGE?
SIDESWIPE—THERE'S NOWHERE ELSE I'D BE.
BRAKKA BRAKKA BRAKKA BRAKKA

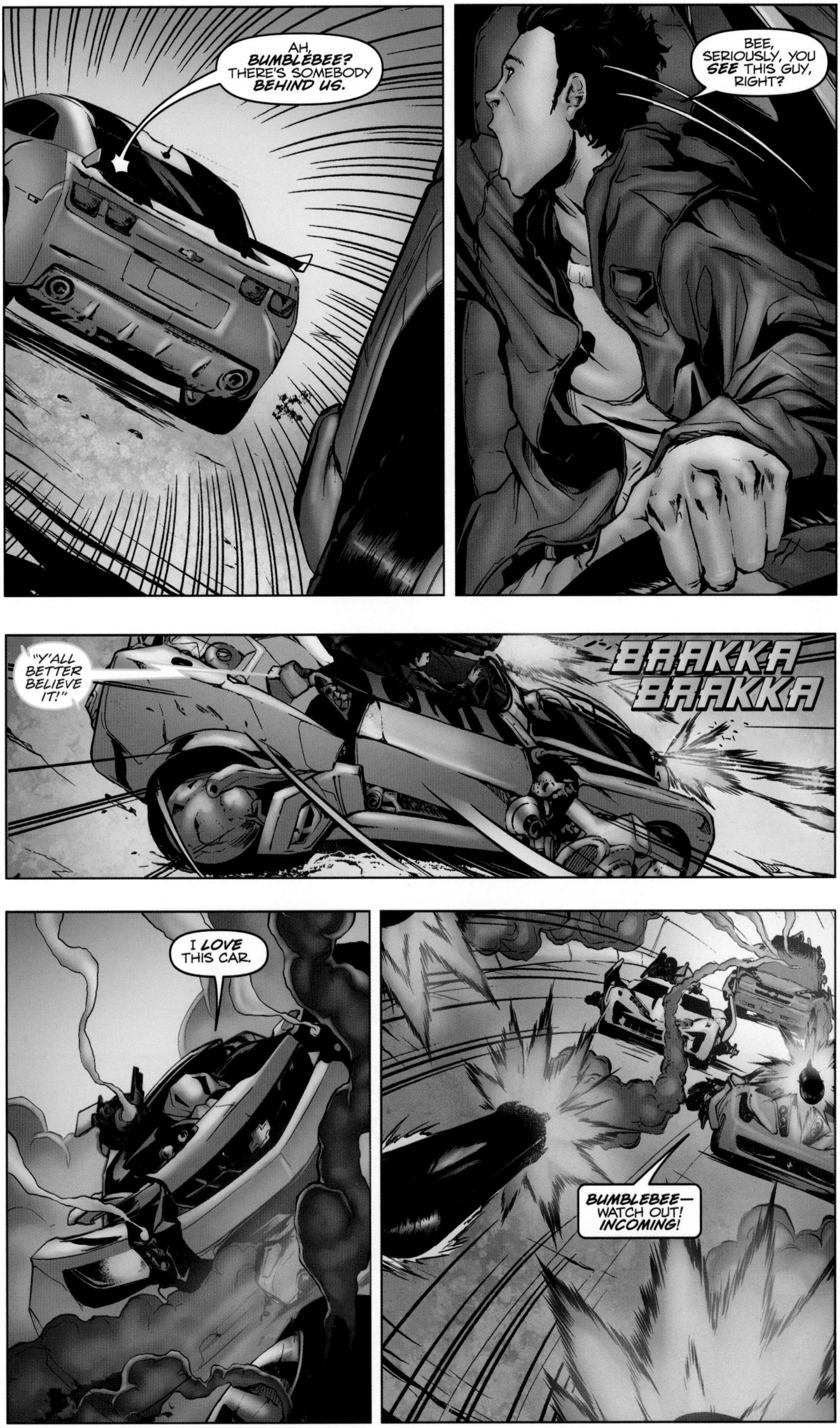
AH, BUMBLEBEE? THERE'S SOMEBODY BEHIND US.
BEE, SERIOUSLY, YOU SEE THIS GUY, RIGHT?
"Y'ALL BETTER BELIEVE IT!"
BRAKKA BRAKKA
I LOVE THIS CAR.
BUMBLEBEE— WATCH OUT! INCOMING!

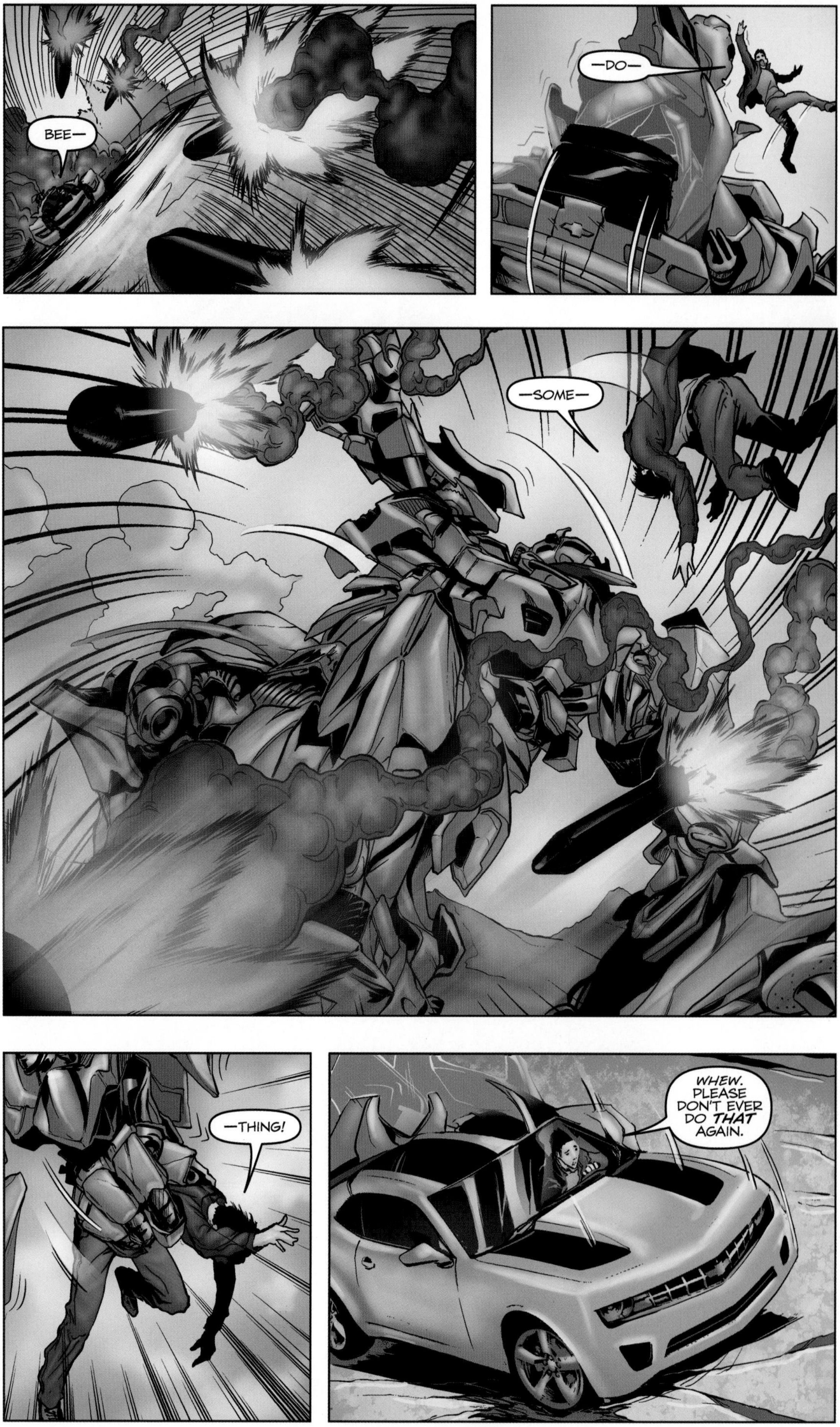
BEE—
—DO—
—SOME—
—THING!
WHEW. PLEASE DON'T EVER DO *THAT* AGAIN.

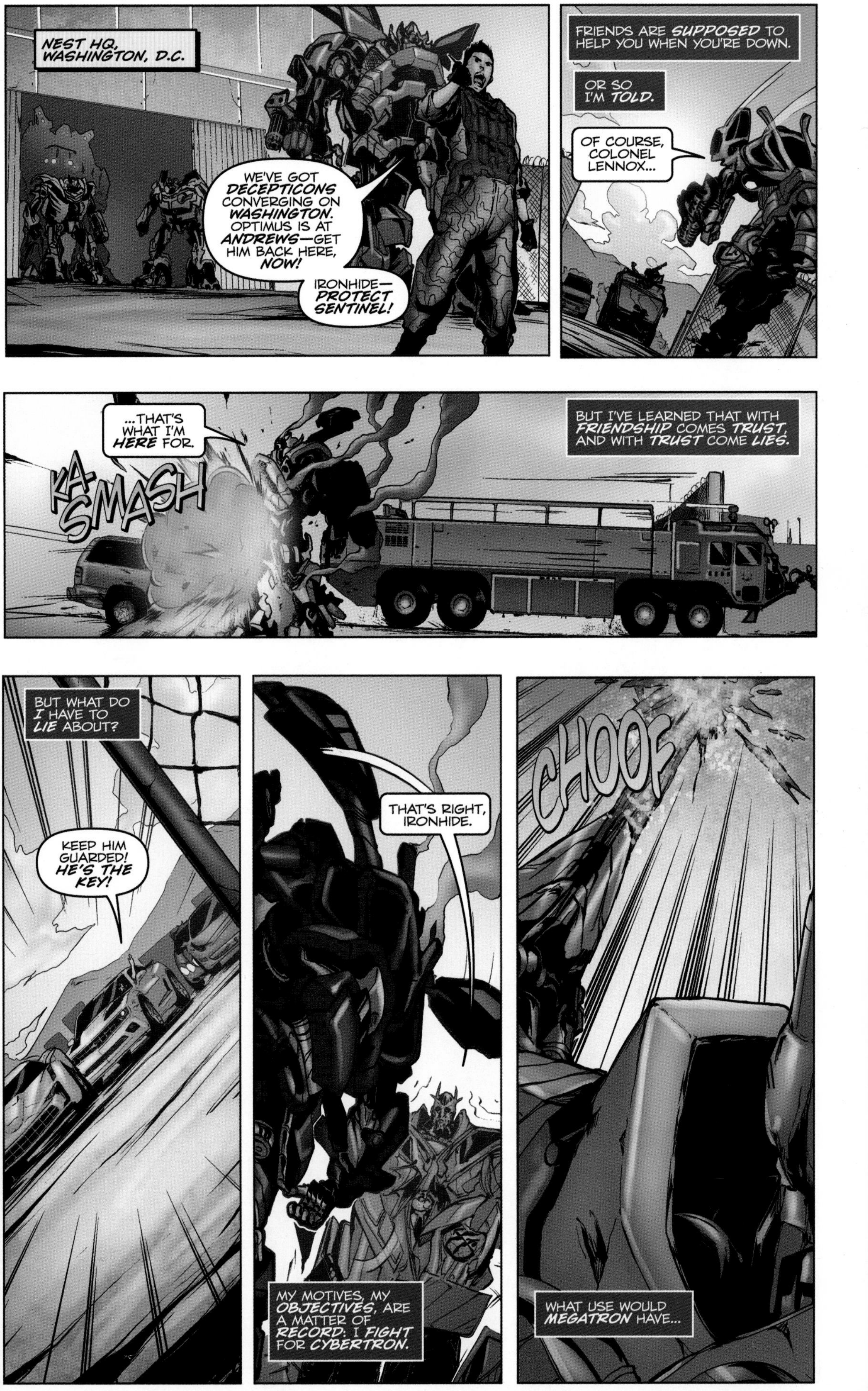

NEST HQ, WASHINGTON, D.C.
WE'VE GOT DECEPTICONS CONVERGING ON WASHINGTON. OPTIMUS IS AT ANDREWS—GET HIM BACK HERE, NOW!
IRONHIDE—PROTECT SENTINEL!
FRIENDS ARE SUPPOSED TO HELP YOU WHEN YOU'RE DOWN.
OR SO I'M TOLD.
OF COURSE, COLONEL LENNOX...
...THAT'S WHAT I'M HERE FOR.
KA SMASH
BUT I'VE LEARNED THAT WITH FRIENDSHIP COMES TRUST, AND WITH TRUST COME LIES.
BUT WHAT DO I HAVE TO LIE ABOUT?
KEEP HIM GUARDED! HE'S THE KEY!
THAT'S RIGHT, IRONHIDE.
MY MOTIVES, MY OBJECTIVES, ARE A MATTER OF RECORD: I FIGHT FOR CYBERTRON.
CHOOF
WHAT USE WOULD MEGATRON HAVE...

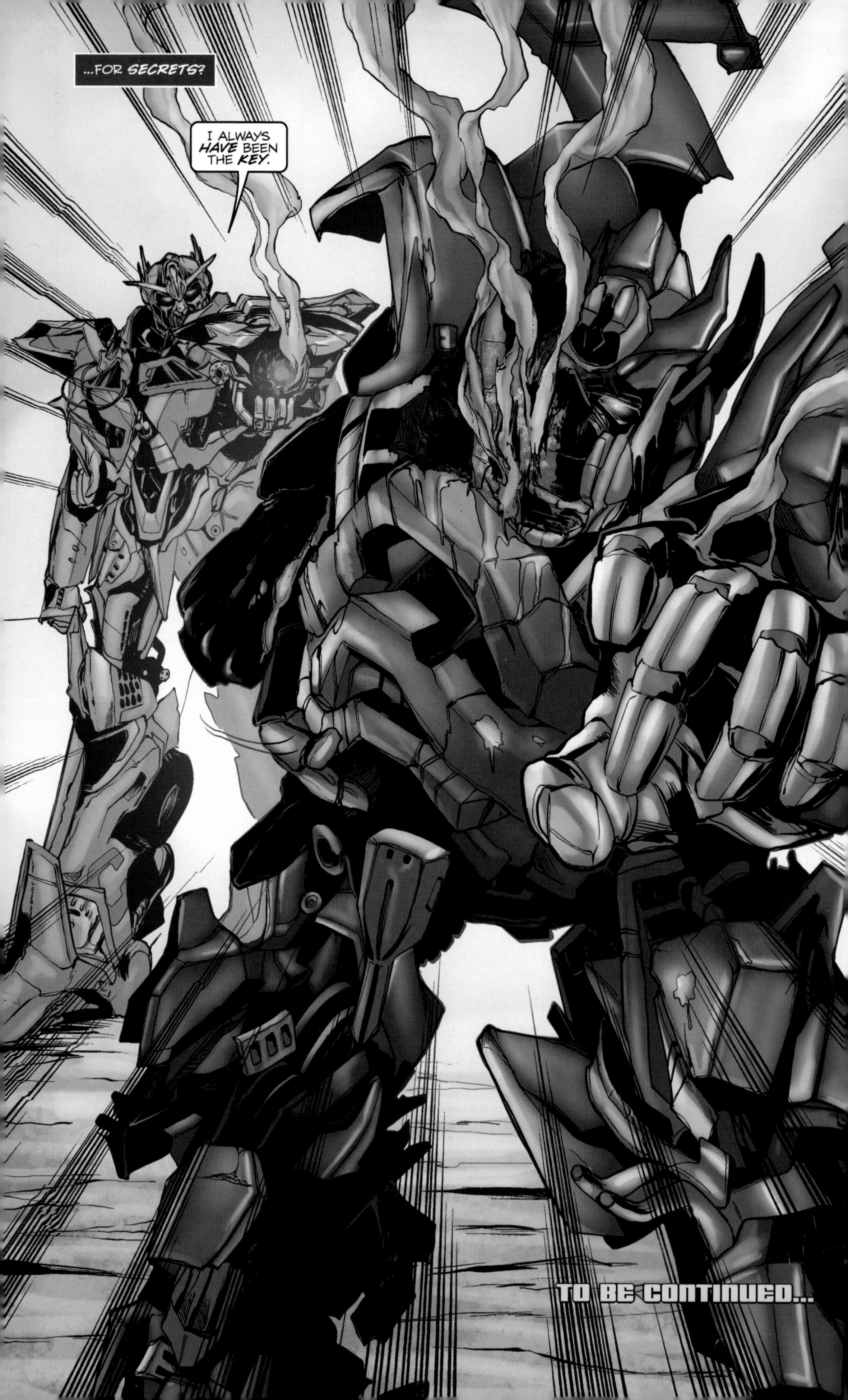
...FOR SECRETS?
I ALWAYS HAVE BEEN THE KEY.
TO BE CONTINUED...